D1761496

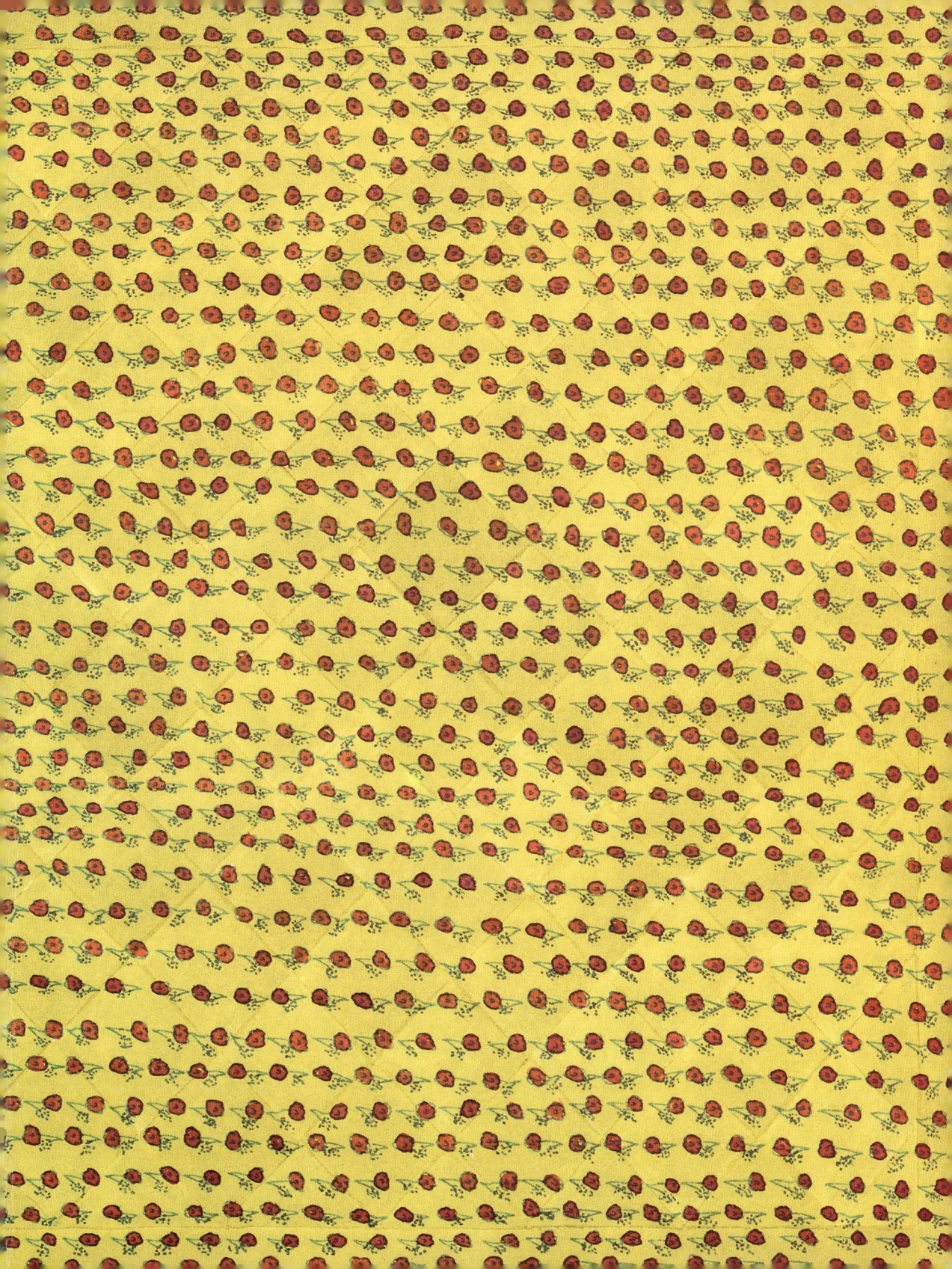

For Nina

PUFFIN BOOKS
Published by the Penguin Group
Penguin Books USA Inc., 375 Hudson Street, New York, New York 10014, U.S.A.
Penguin Books Ltd, 27 Wrights Lane, London W8 5TZ, England
Penguin Books Australia Ltd, Ringwood, Victoria, Australia
Penguin Books Canada Ltd, 10 Alcorn Avenue, Toronto, Ontario, Canada M4V 3B2
Penguin Books (N.Z.) Ltd, 182-190 Wairau Road, Auckland 10, New Zealand

Penguin Books Ltd, Registered Offices: Harmondsworth, Middlesex, England

First published in the United States of America by Greenwillow Books,
a division of William Morrow & Company, Inc., 1984
Reprinted by arrangement with William Morrow & Company, Inc.
Published in Puffin Books, 1994

10 9 8 7 6 5 4 3 2 1

Copyright © Ann Jonas, 1984
All rights reserved

LIBRARY OF CONGRESS CATALOGING-IN-PUBLICATION DATA
Jonas, Ann.
The quilt / Ann Jonas. p. cm.
Summary: A child's new patchwork quilt recalls old memories and
provides new adventures at bedtime.
[1. Quilts—Fiction. 2. Bedtime—Fiction. 3. Afro-Americans—Fiction.] I. Title.
PZ7.J664Qi 1994 [E]—dc20 93-46684 CIP AC

ISBN 0-14-055308-8

Printed in the United States of America

Except in the United States of America, this book is sold subject to the condition that
it shall not, by way of trade or otherwise, be lent, re-sold, hired out, or otherwise
circulated without the publisher's prior consent in any form of binding or cover
other than that in which it is published and without a similar condition
including this condition being imposed on the subsequent purchaser.

The Quilt
Ann Jonas
PUFFIN BOOKS

I have a new quilt.

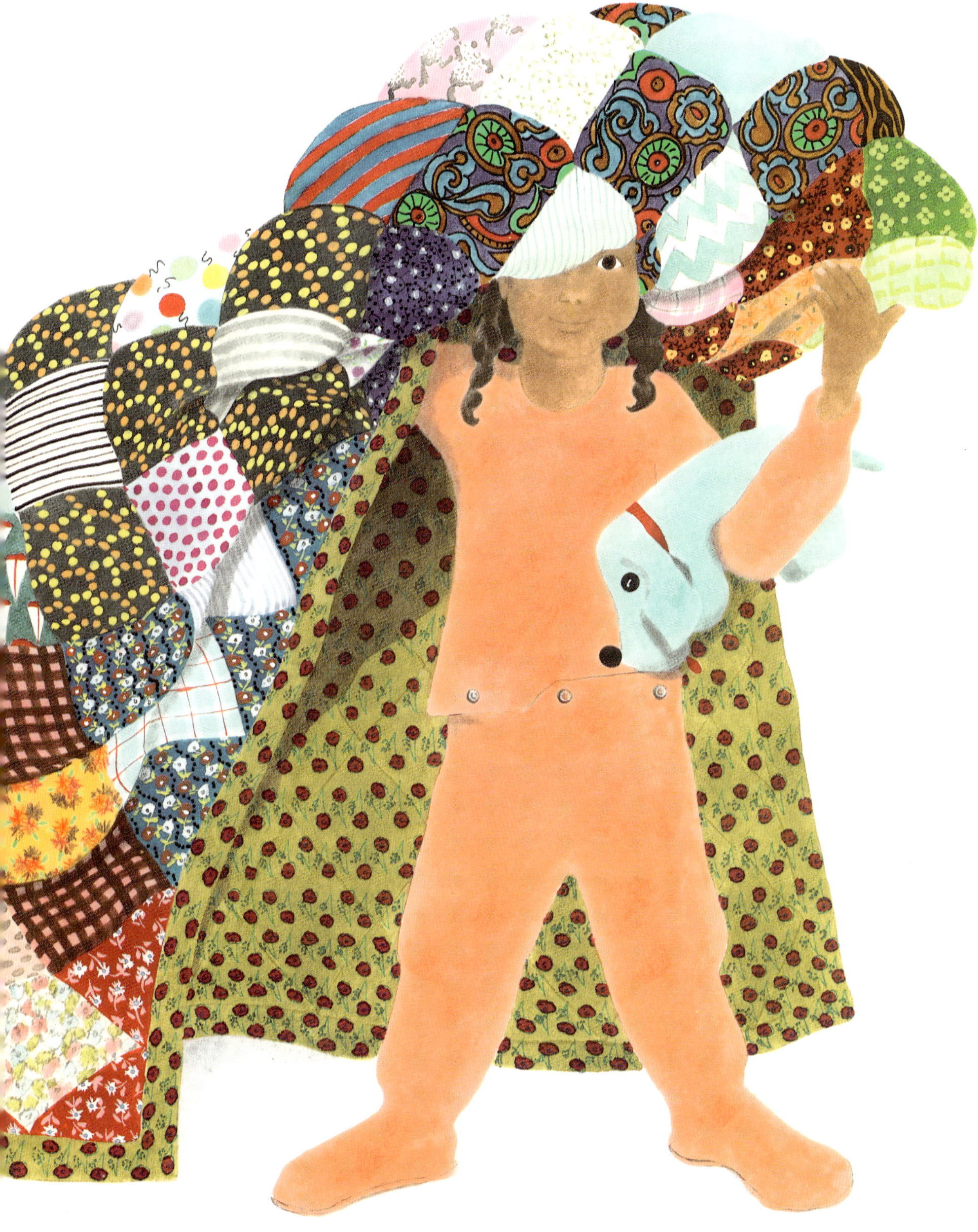

It's to go on my
new grown-up bed.

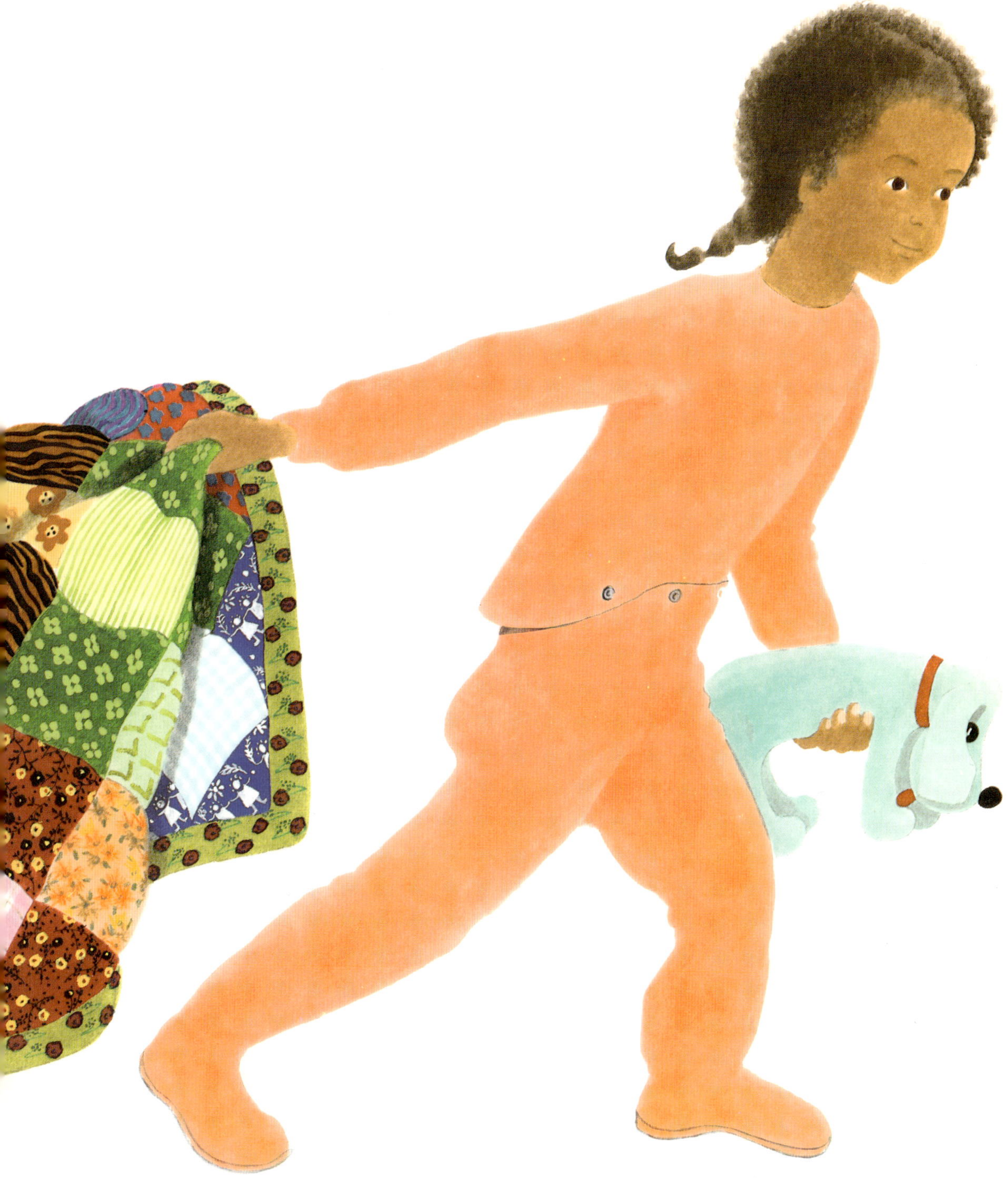

My mother and father made it for me. They used some of my old things. Here are my first curtains and my crib sheet. Sally is lying on my baby pajamas.

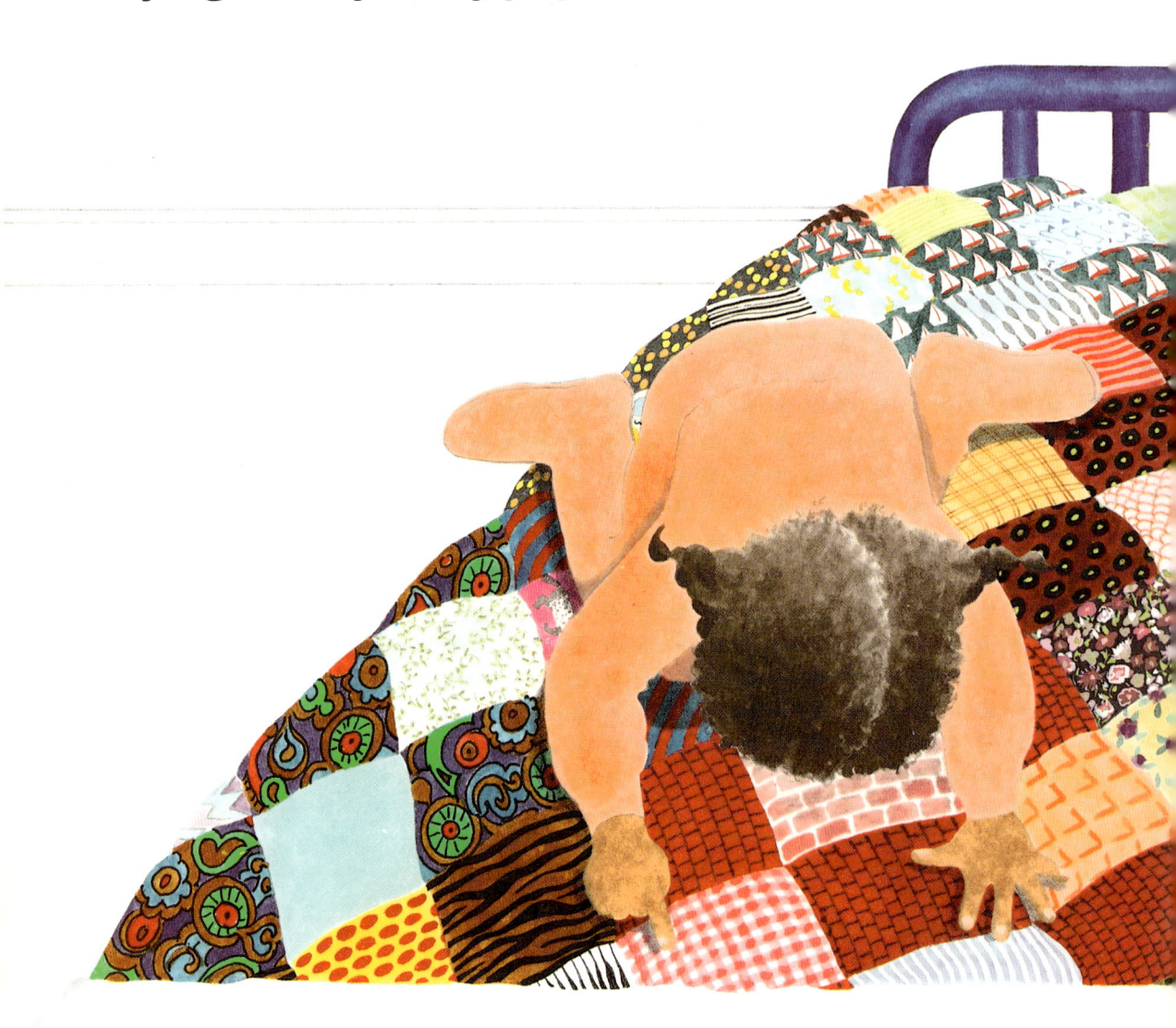

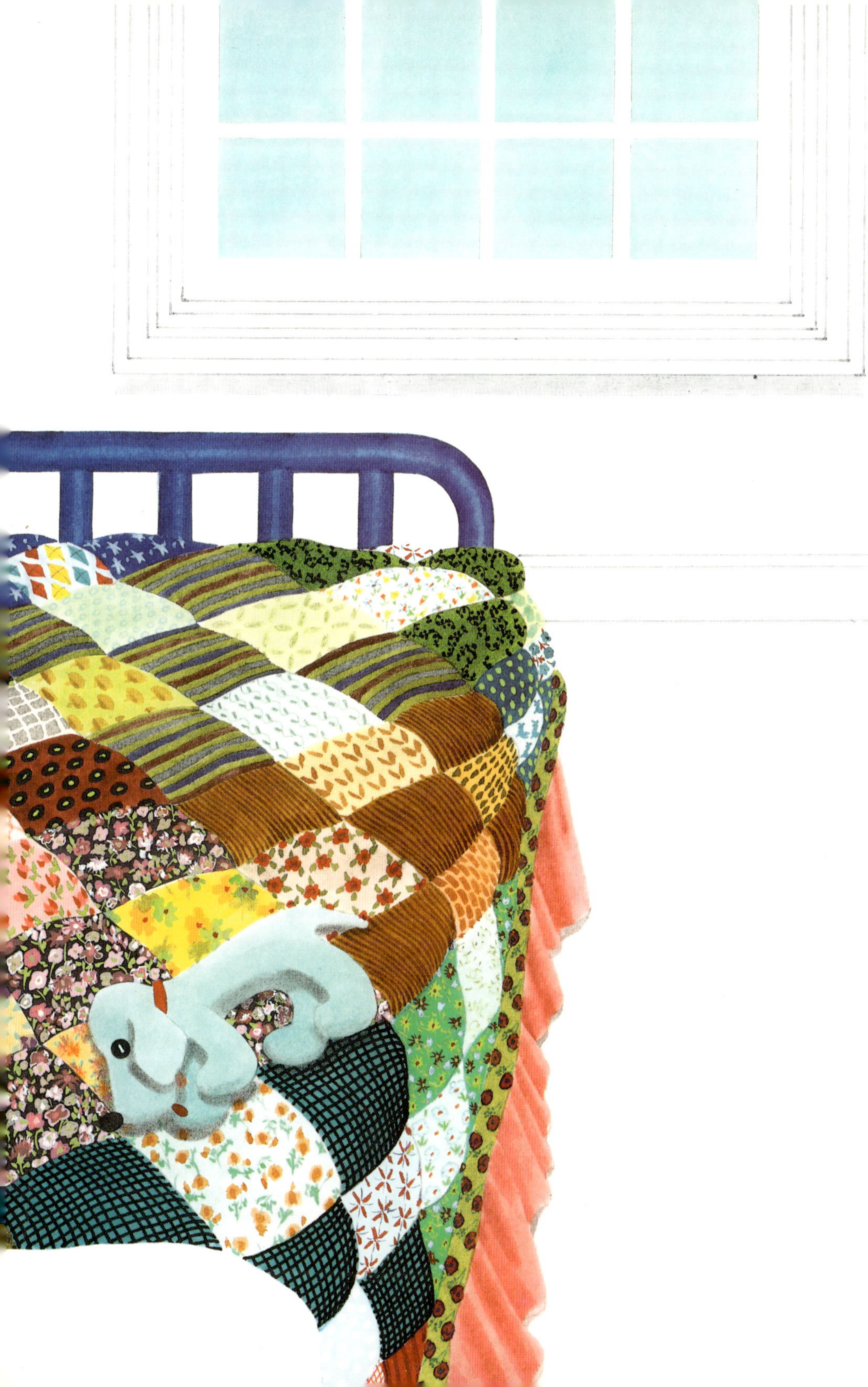

That's the shirt I wore on my second birthday. This piece is from my favorite pants. They got too small. The cloth my mother used to make Sally is here somewhere. I can't find it now.

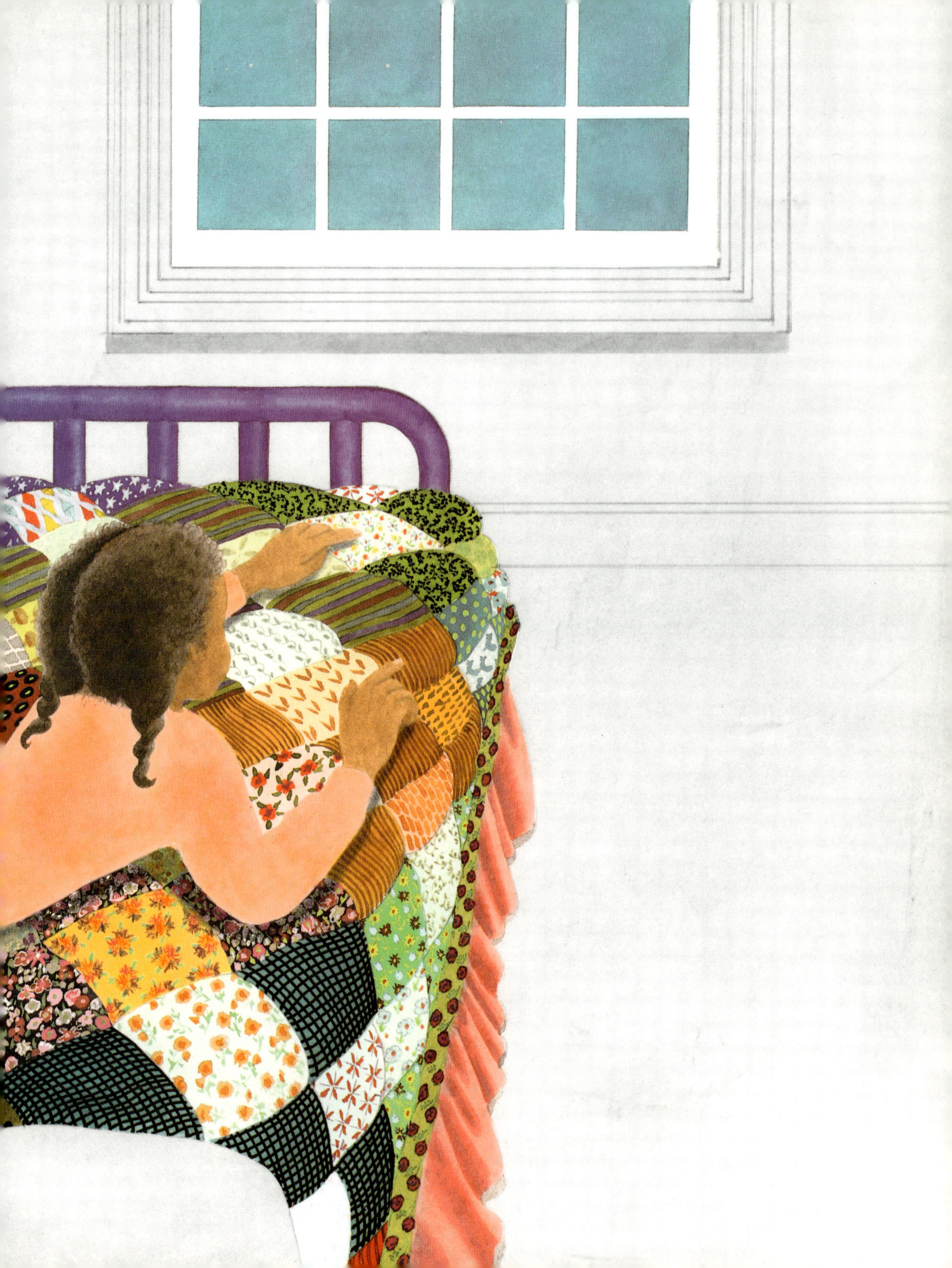

I know I won't be able
to go to sleep tonight.

It almost looks
like a little town....

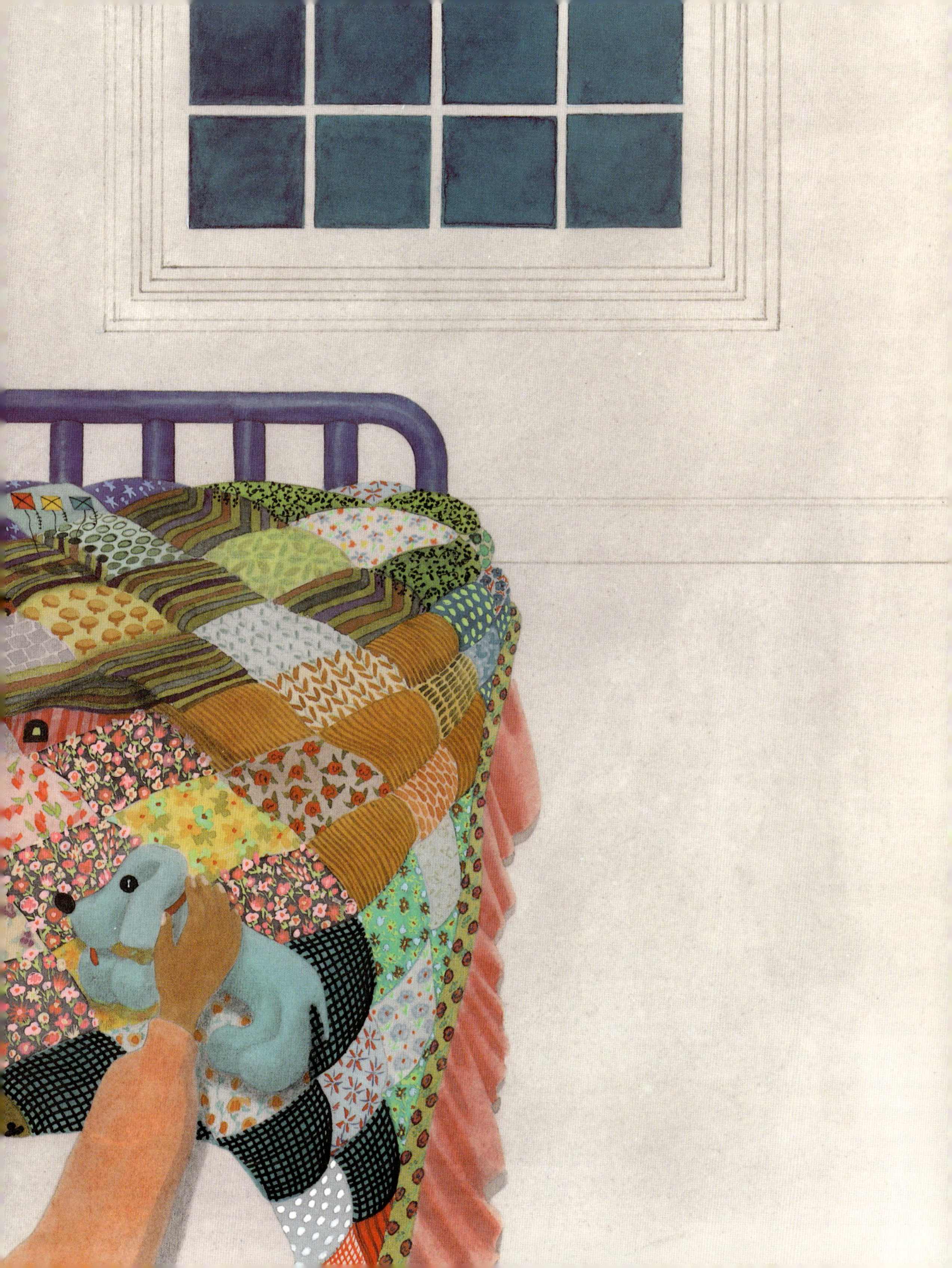

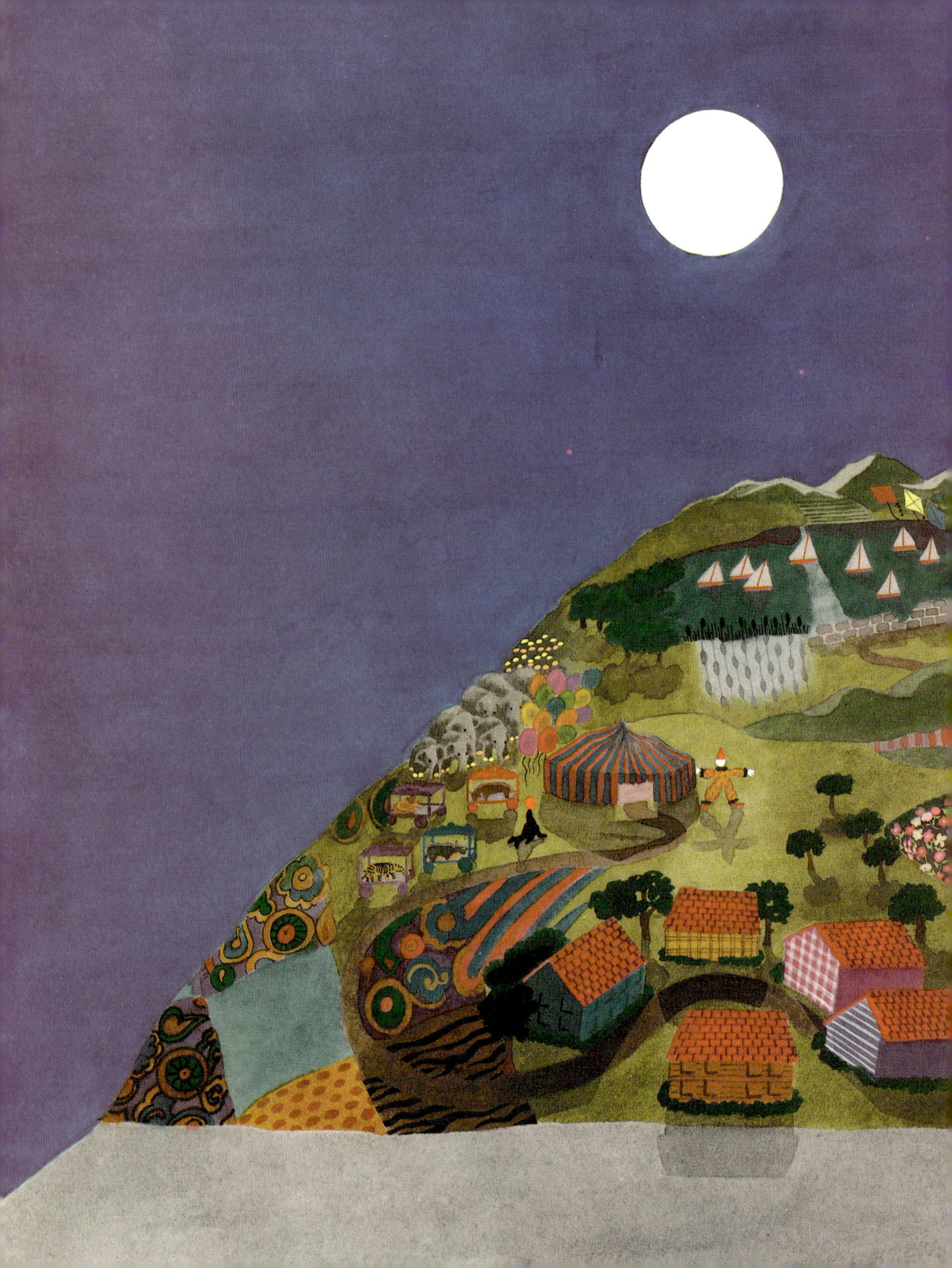

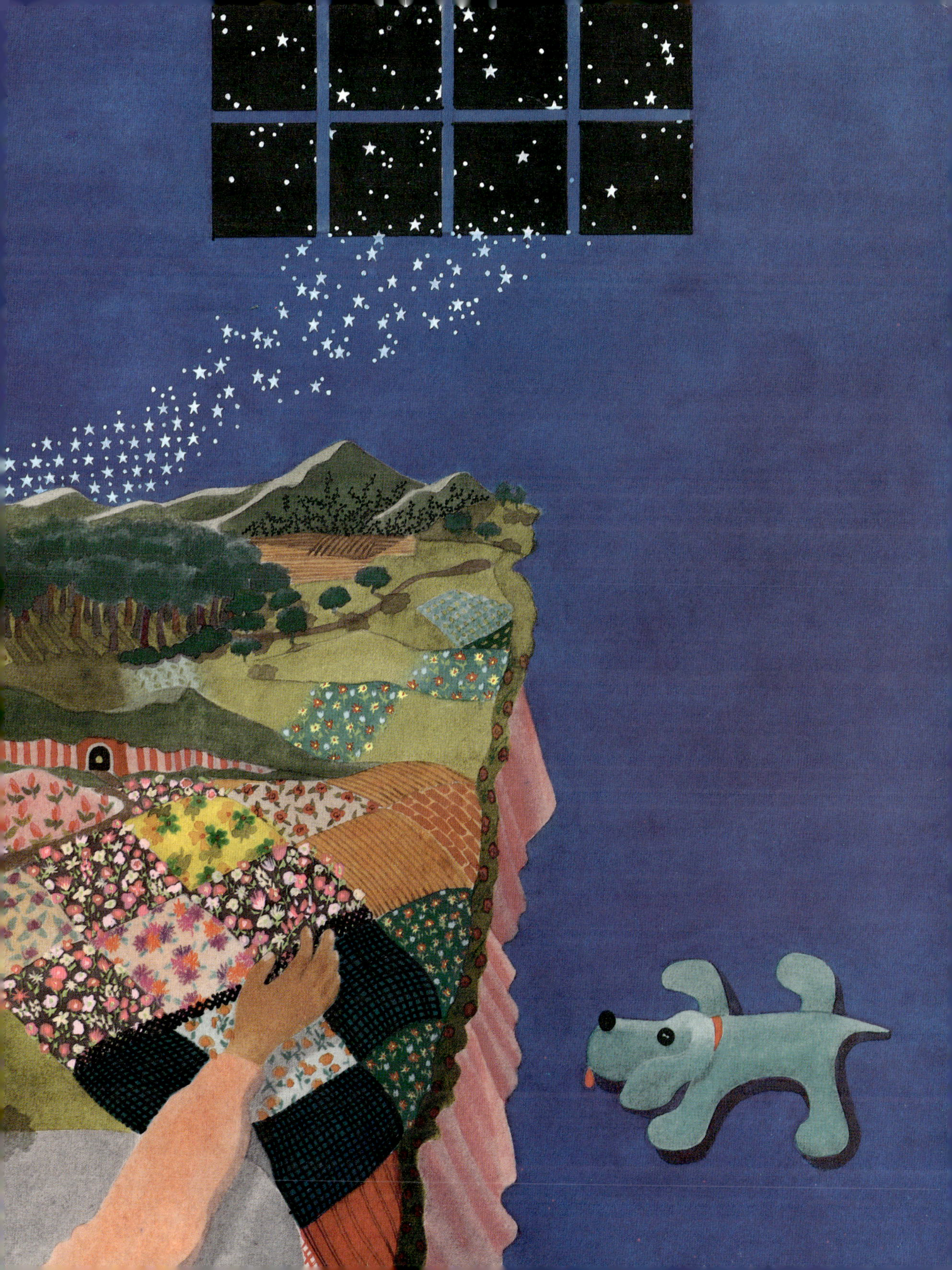

I can't find Sally!

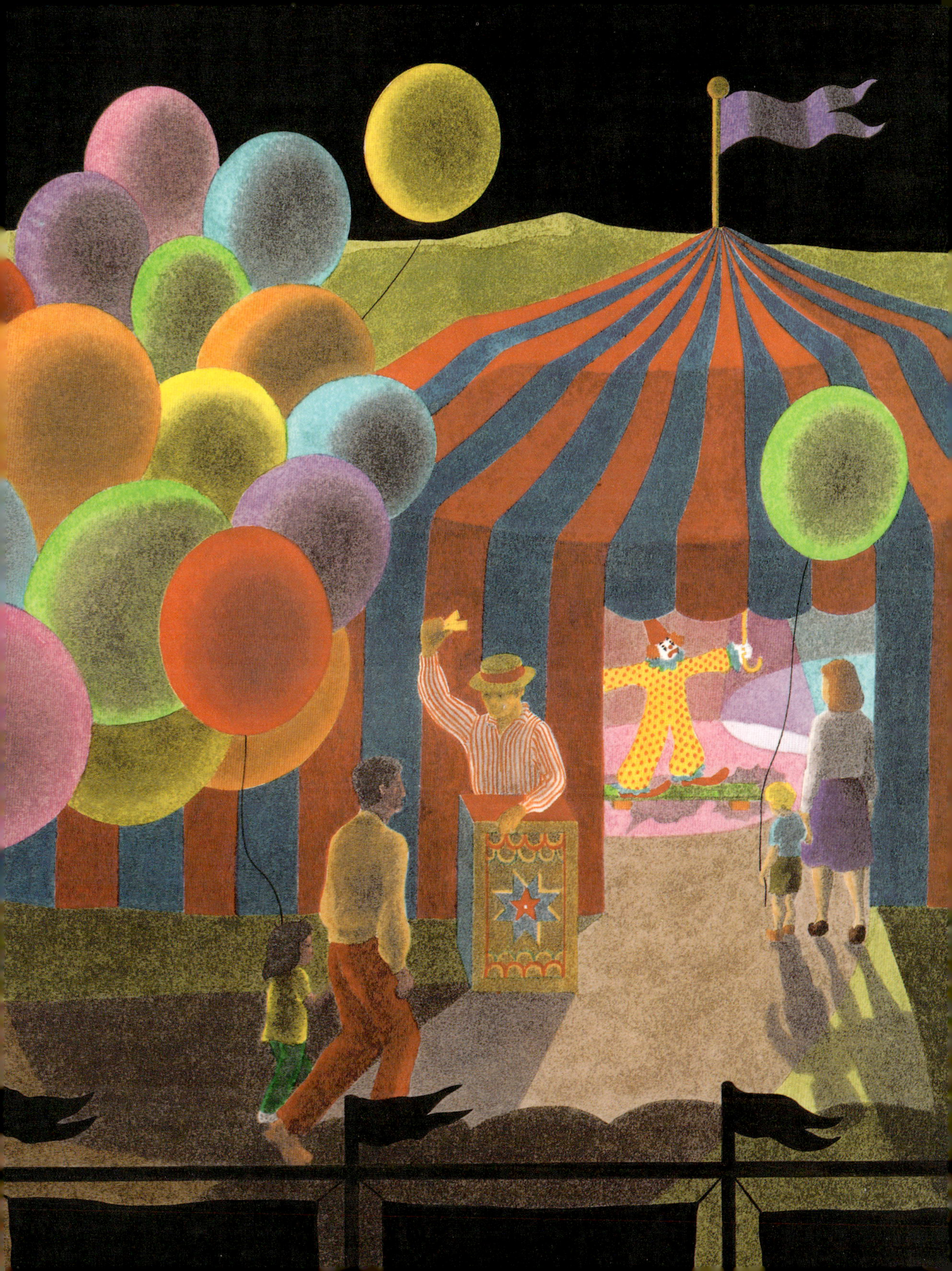

Maybe she's here. Sally!

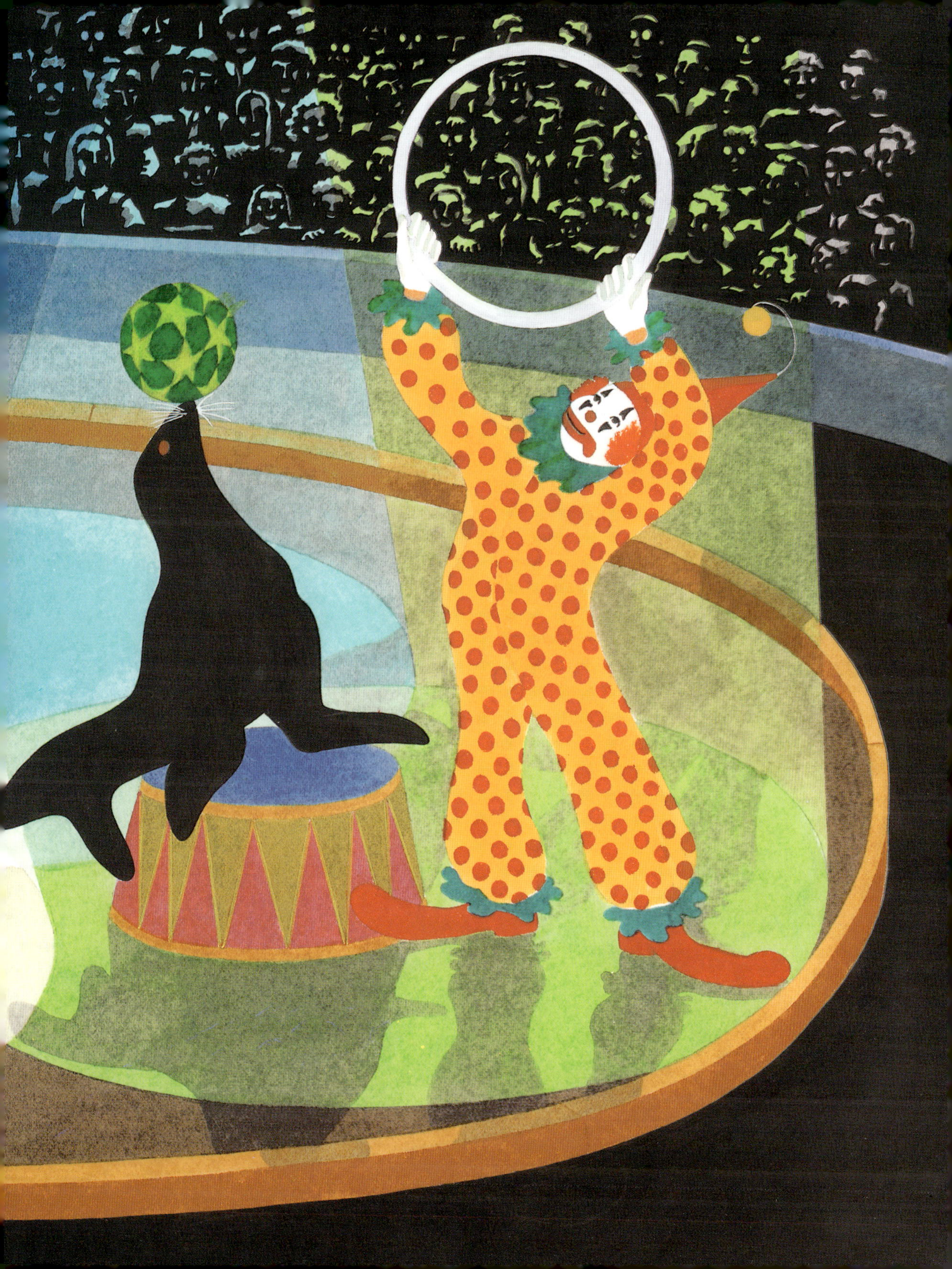

She wouldn't like it here. Sally!

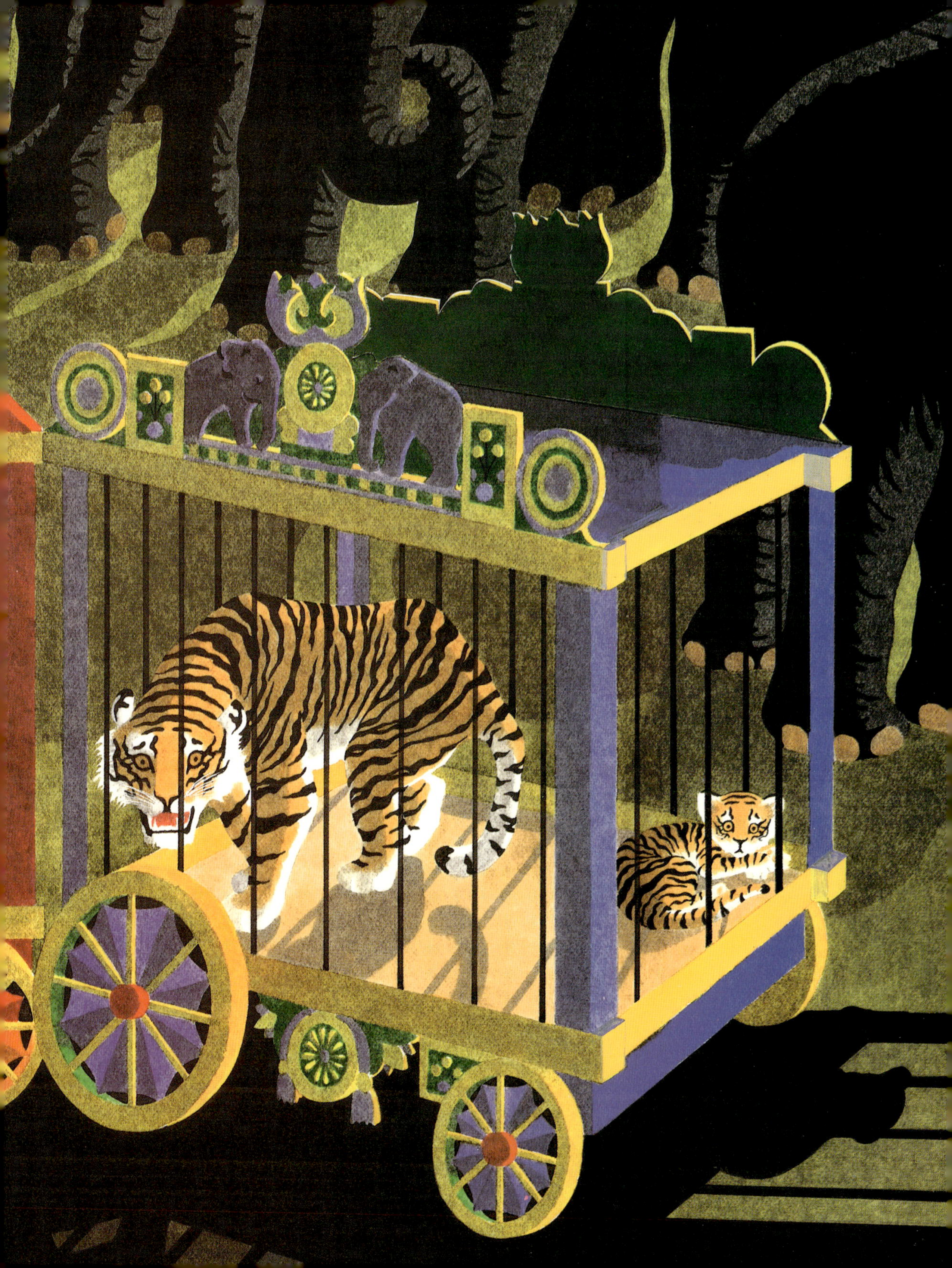

What if someone took her home? Sally!

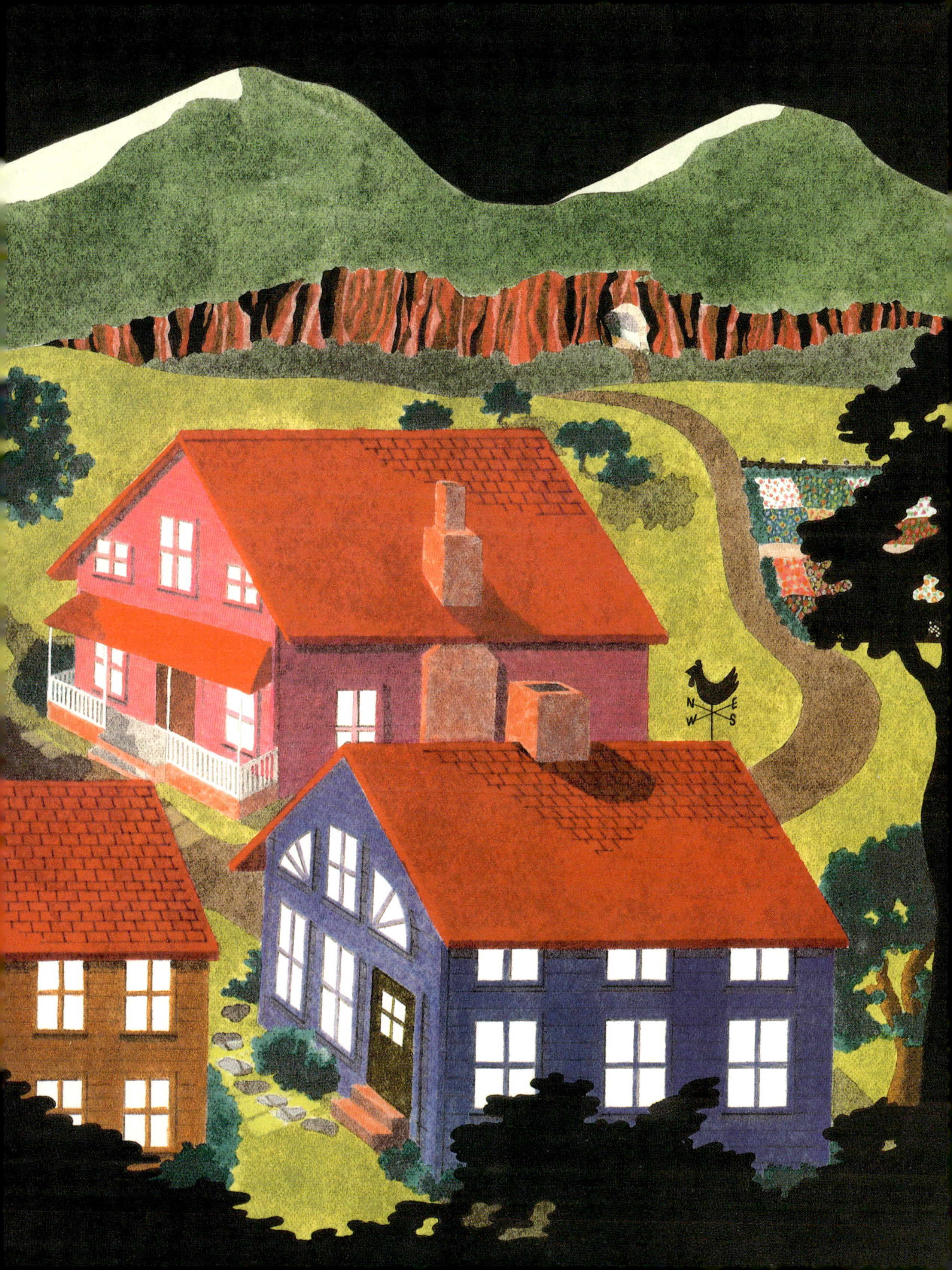
N
E
W
S

If she hid here,
I'd never find her.
Sally!

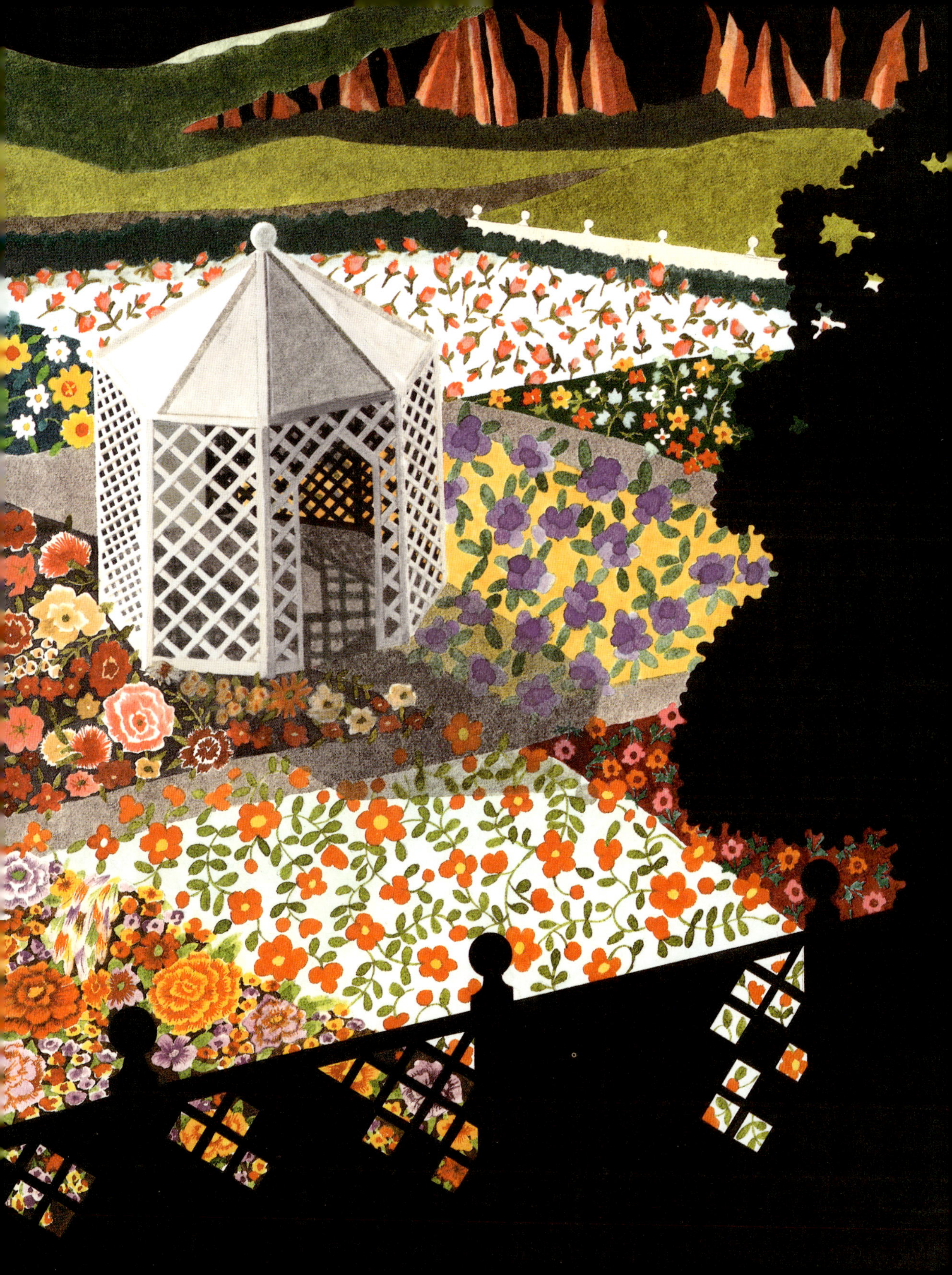

What a scary tunnel!
I'll run through fast.
Sally! Sally! Sally!
Sally! Sally! Sally!

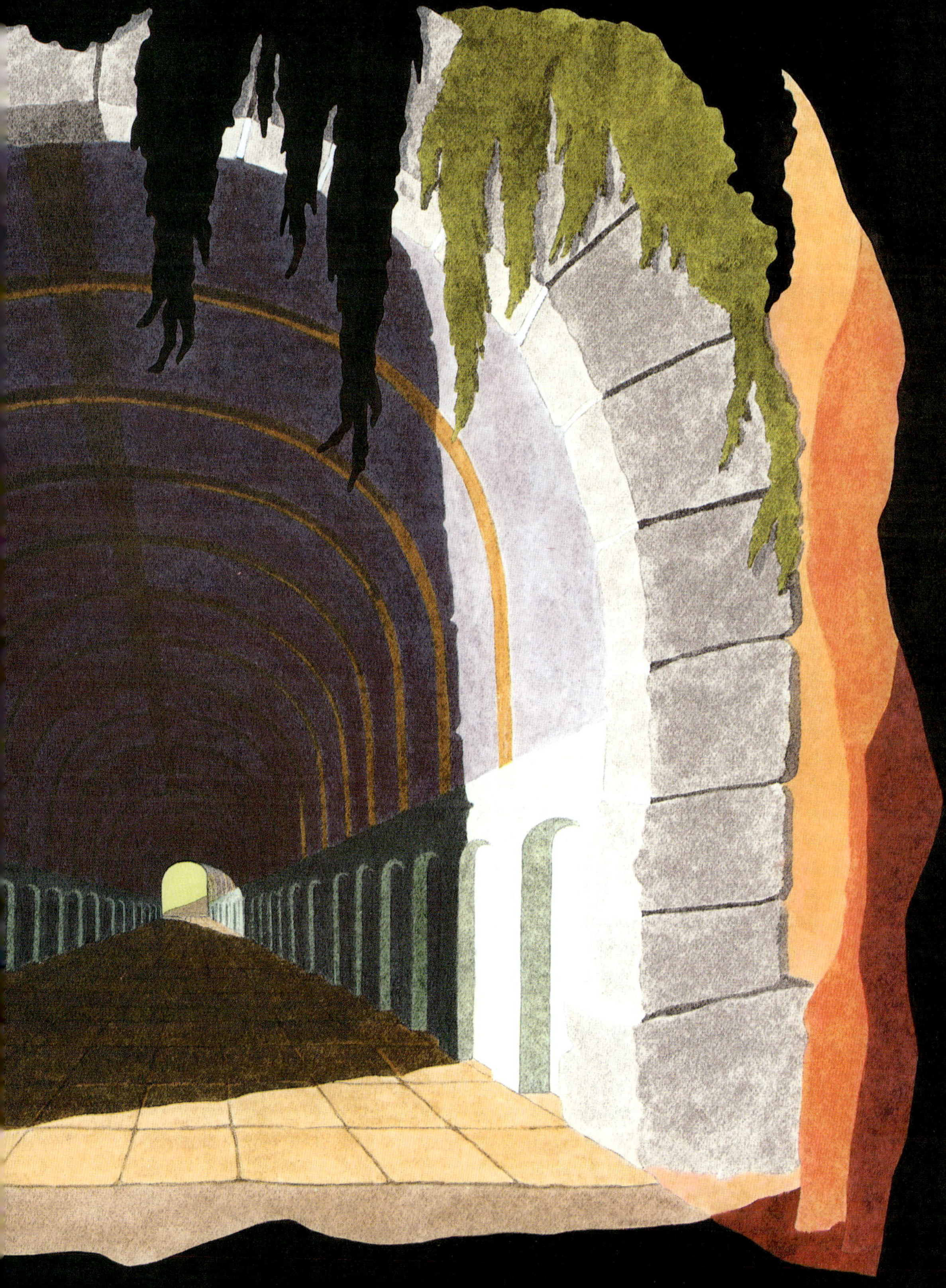

She wouldn't be here.
She doesn't like water.
Sally!

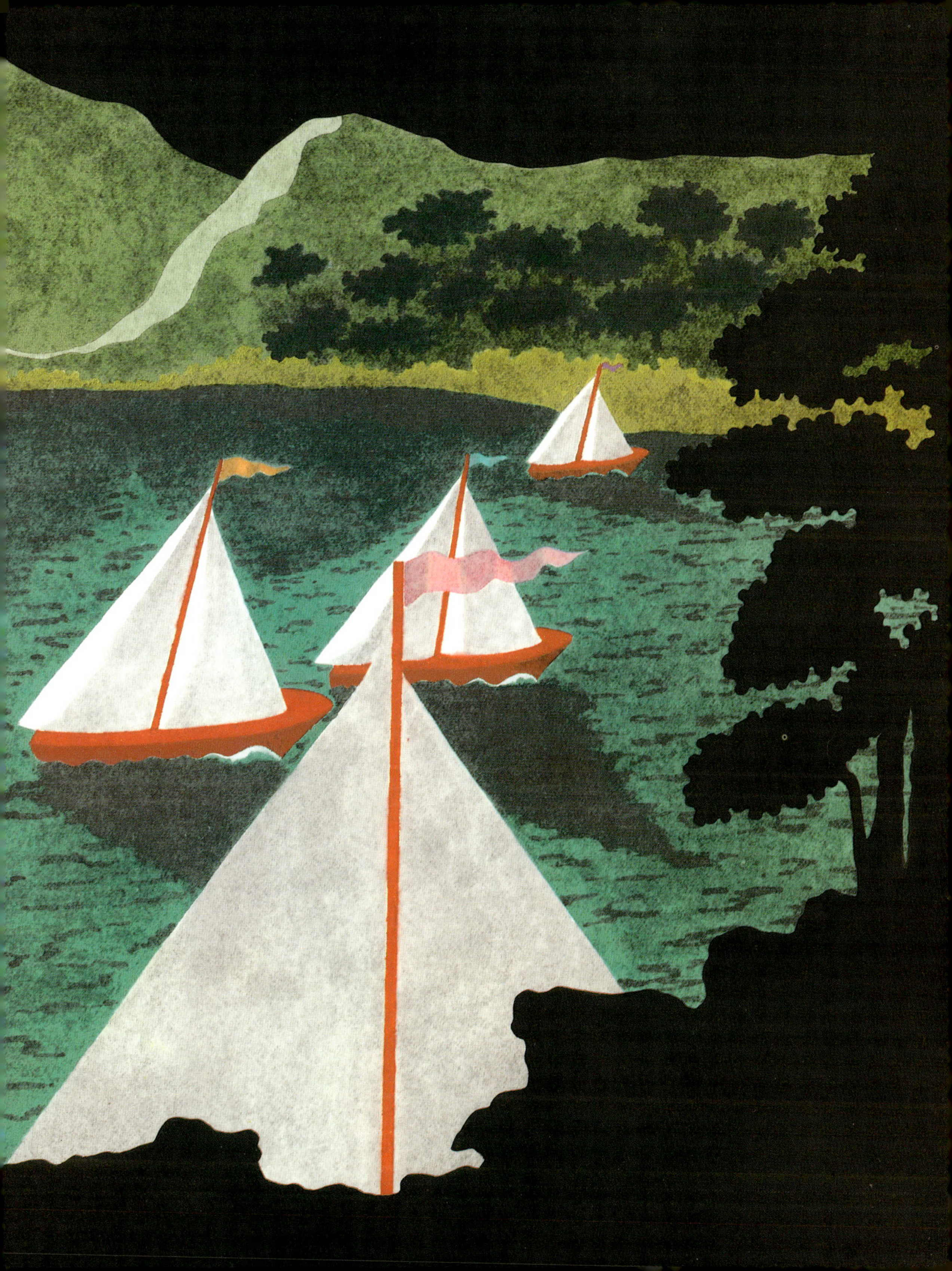

This is worse than the tunnel! Sally!

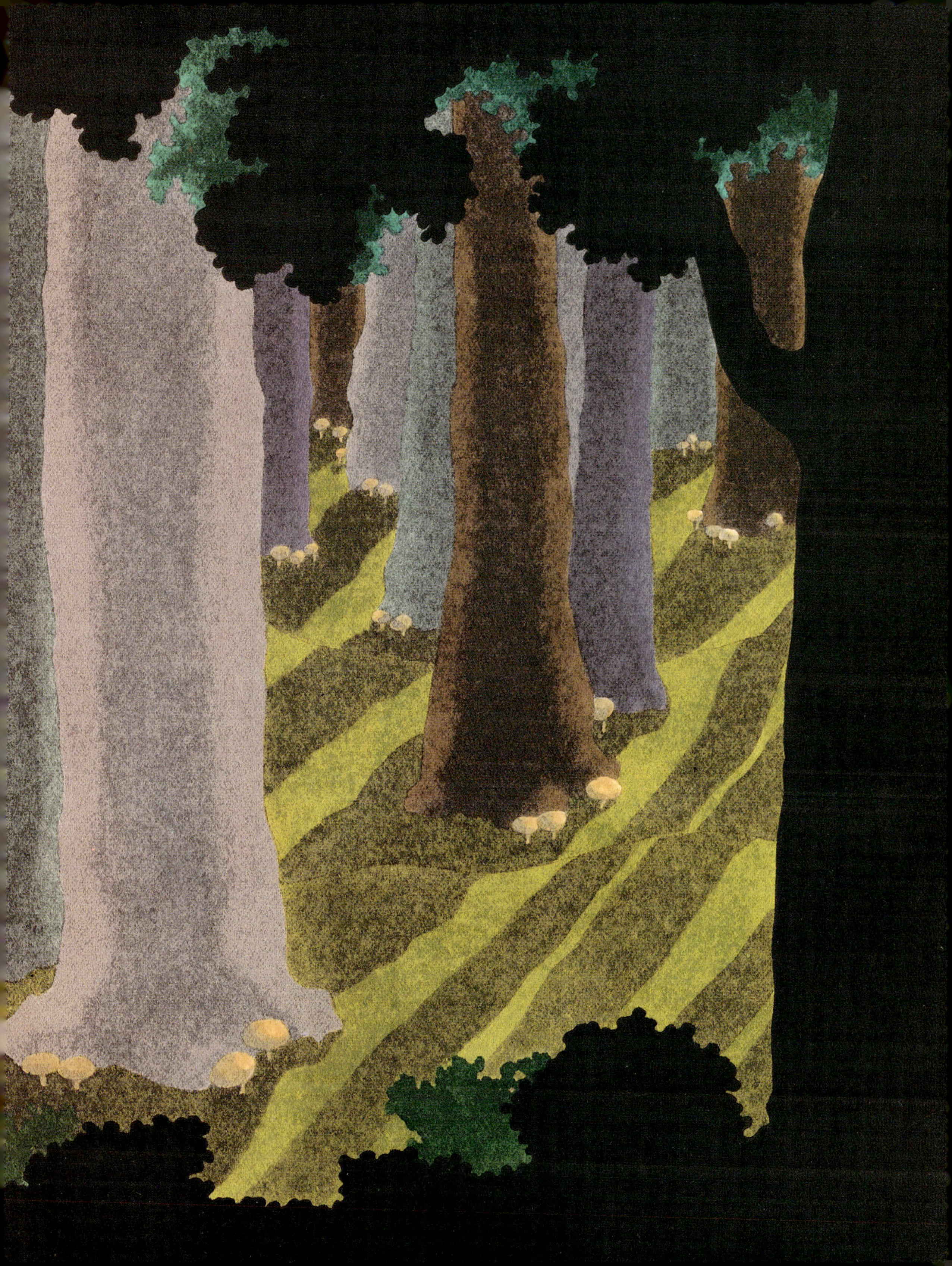

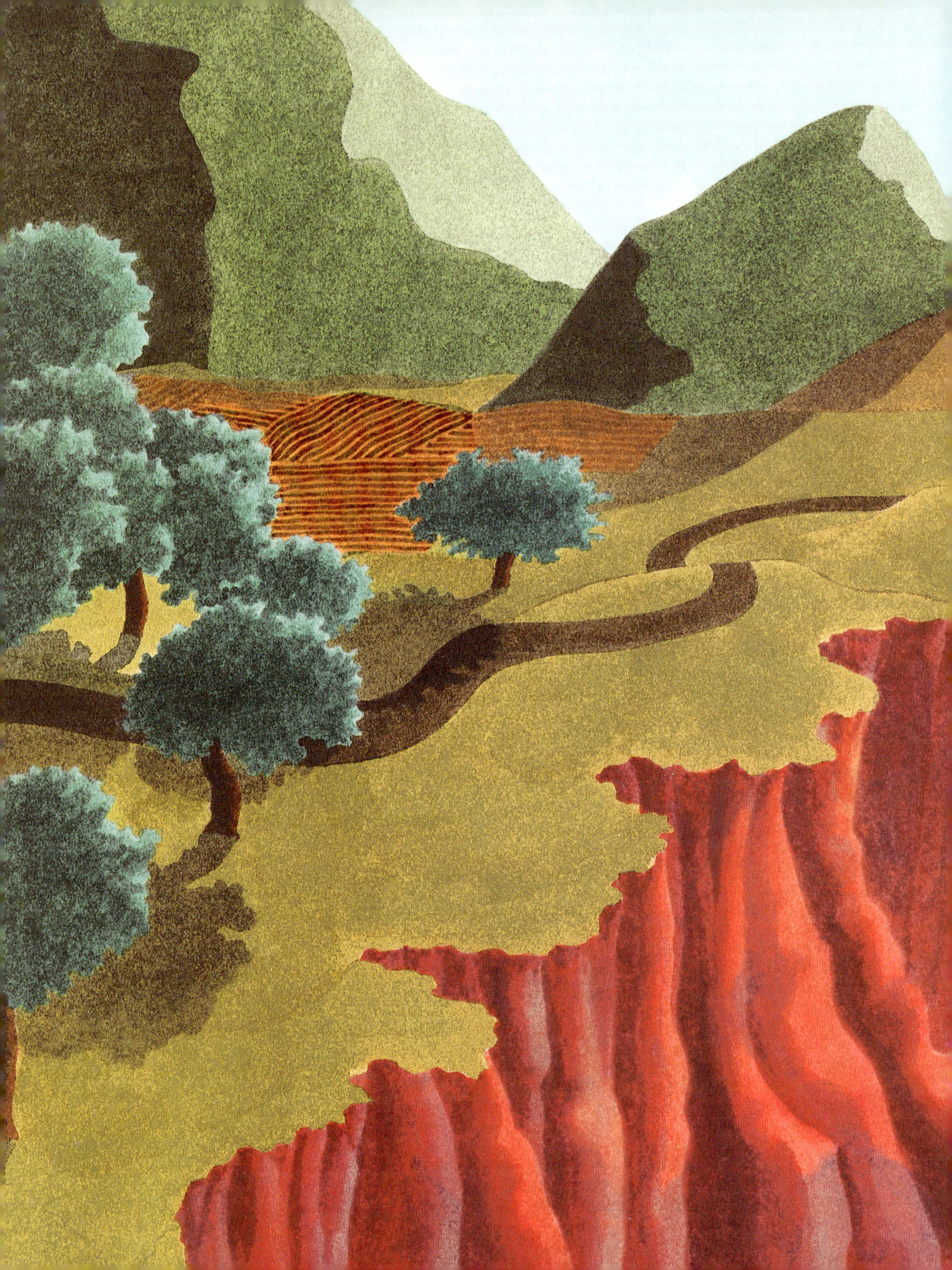

I see her!

Good morning, Sally.

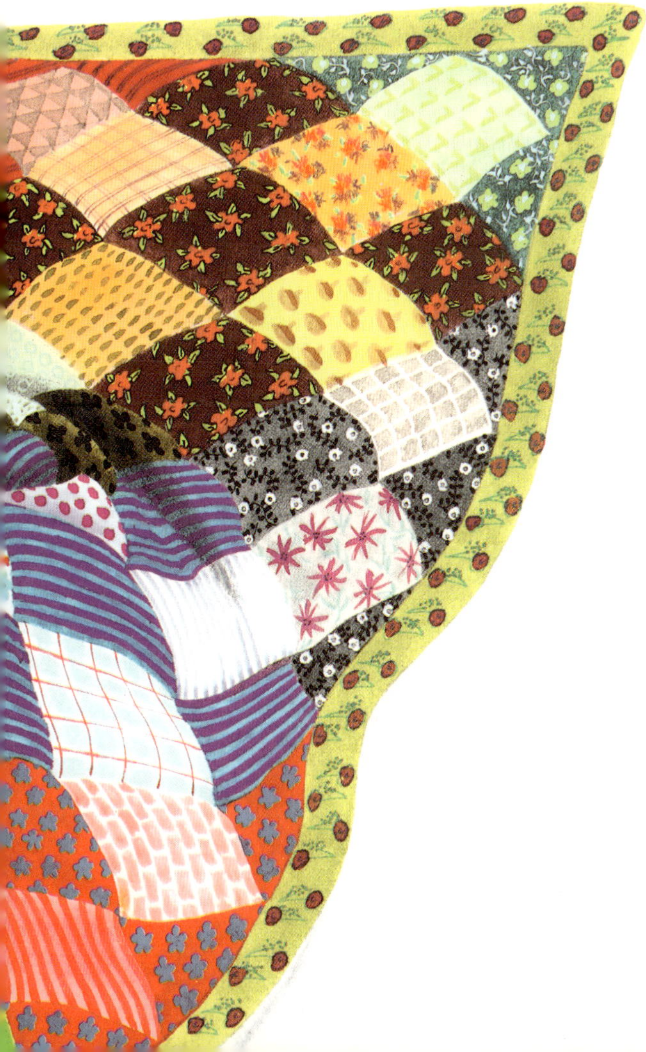

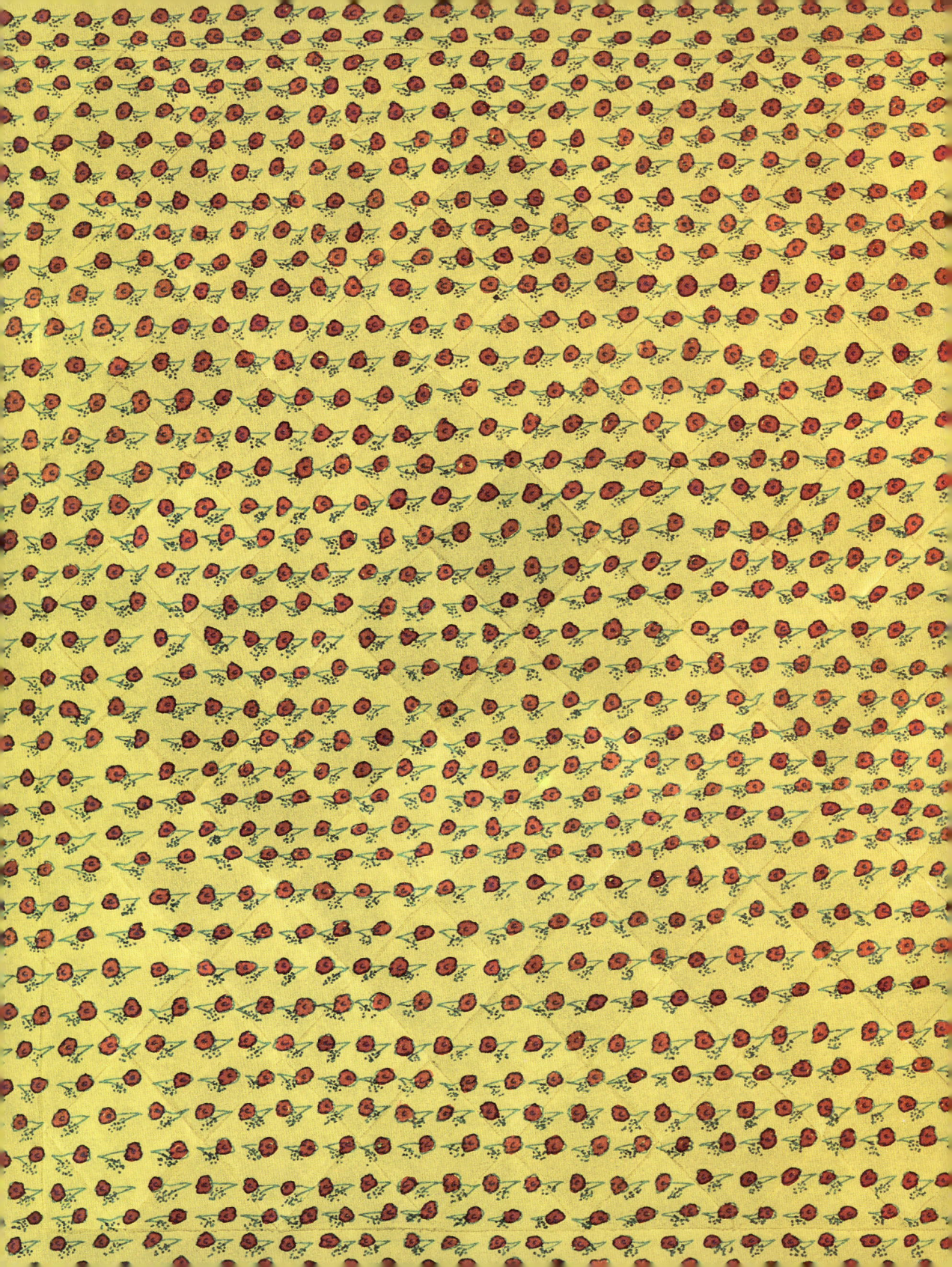

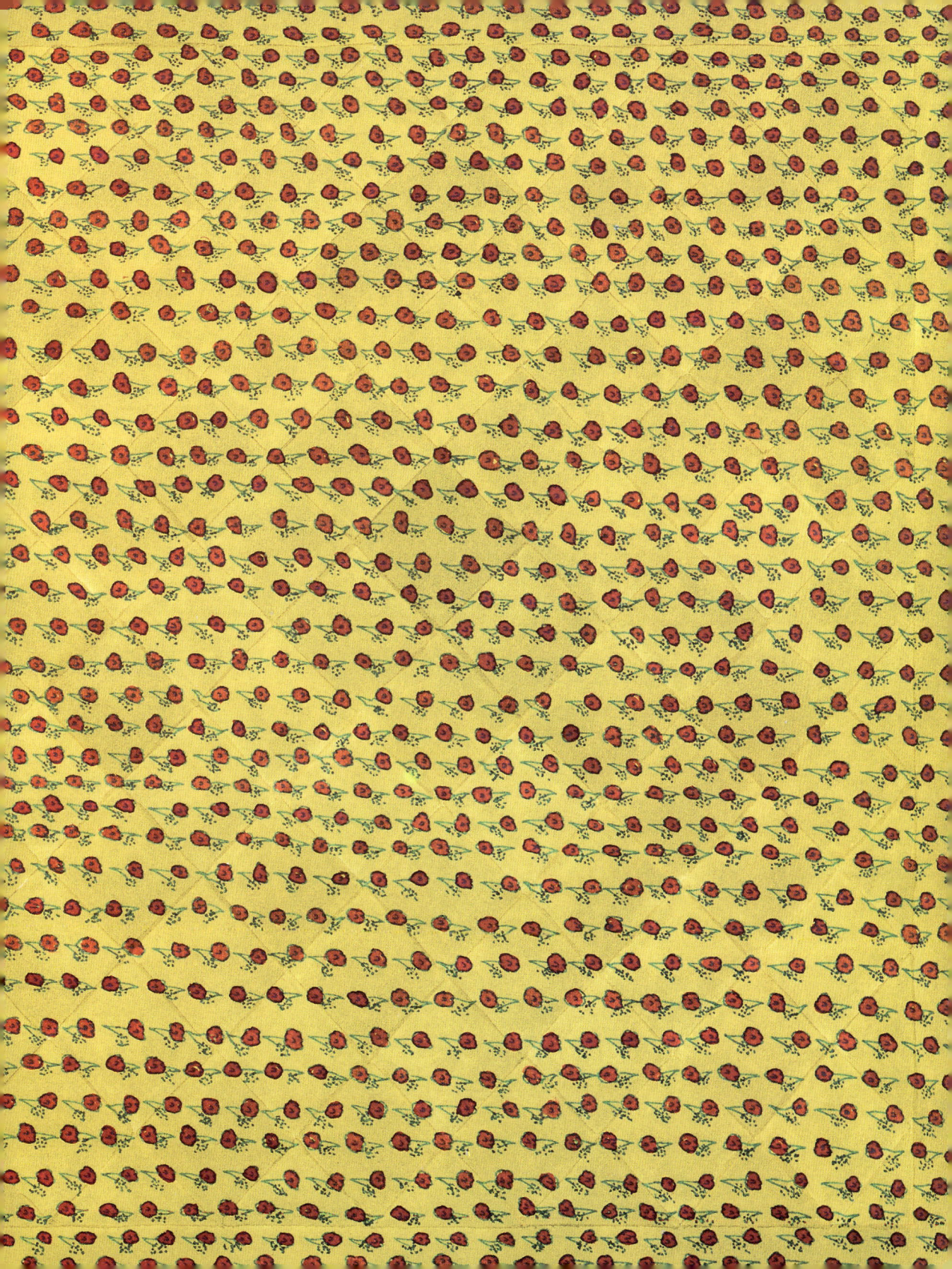